MATH FOR THE SELF-CRIPPLING

STORIES

URSULA VILLARREAL-MOURA

GOLD LINE PRESS

Copyright© 2022 by Ursula Villarreal-Moura
All rights reserved
Cover and Book design : Sandra Rosales
Published : Gold Line Press
http://goldlinepress.com
Gold Line titles are distributed by Small Press Distributions
This title is also available for purchase directly from the publisher
www.spdbooks.org : 800.869.7553
Library of Congress Cataloging-in-Publication Data
Math for the Self-Crippling / Ursula Villarreal-Moura
Library of Congress Control Number 2022932104
Villarreal-Moura, Ursula
ISBN 978-1-938900-42-6

*For Dominga B. Laque, Celestina Benavidez,
and Daniel S. Laque*

TABLE OF CONTENTS

ENVELOPE FIRST, 1953 • 1

ORIGIN, 1983 • 2

OF PESADILLAS, 1987 • 5

FATIMA, MIDSTRIDE, CIRCA 1988 • 6

ONE EARRING • 8

BLOOD PAISLEYS, 1990 • 11

SAD GIRL, 1992 • 13

THROUGH SOPHIA LOREN GLASSES • 16

RUBRIC FOR YOUR NEW ENGLAND COLLEGE EXPERIENCE, 1998 • 19

HUNGRY PARALLELOGRAM • 21

COASTAL CUNEIFORM • 23

FUR OF MY INSECURITIES • 25

TABLOID TOTEMS • 28

HANDS ON METALLIC PONDS • 30

SHORT ANSWERS • 32

LAST CHAPTER ON HOTEL STATIONERY • 34

THE EQUIVALENT OF _____ • 38

MACROSCOPIC SACRED PUZZLES • 41

THE POSTURE OF A GENTLEMAN • 42

EFFIGIES OF OURSELVES • 44

MUIR BEACH • 46

MATH FOR THE SELF-CRIPPLING • 48

HUSBAND IN TRANSLATION • 50

MASTERPIECES • 52

ABACUS OF SELF-IMPROVEMENT • 53

ENVELOPE FIRST, 1953

A ring of adults holding hands, burning candles, chanting. A series of levitations visible through the window—Tía Veronica claims she and Mama witnessed a séance from their cousin's backyard.

Inside the living room, their frumpy aunts, half-drunk uncles, parents, and strangers summoned spirits with one synchronized hum. First, an envelope floated off the table, then the gingham tablecloth spun off in a gust. Finally, the table bobbed as if riding a cosmic wave.

Fried chicken and white biscuits Tía Veronica and Mama agree is what they ate for dinner that night. Thighs and a twilight game of jacks or hide-and-seek, depending on whom you believe.

The levitations, Mama refutes. When asked to explain them, she shrugs. Her tightened shoulders suggest a mental ruse, a hologram of boredom.

ORIGIN, 1983

I crunched into a buñuelo and stared at my great-aunt Fatima and Grandma Beatrix from across the dining room table. Mid-afternoon sunlight poured through the window, causing each grain of sugar to shine like diamond dust coating my dessert.

"When we were your age, our mother would ask us to go outside and catch grasshoppers," Fatima began in Spanish, adjusting her oversized purple glasses. "Your grandmother and I would take a tin can and return with it full of grasshoppers. Isn't that right, Beatrix?"

Grandma Beatrix nodded with a sly smirk as if remembering something devious.

I lifted the buñuelo and took two more bites. I had no idea in which direction the story was headed, but already I was suspicious of how it would end. Part of being a child was deciding which stories were based in fact and which were simply tales.

"When we gave the can to our mother, she shooed us out of the kitchen. She had spells to cast, secret spells. So, we

ORIGIN, 1983

ran outside to play until we were called back."

"Our family spoke Spanish, and our three older brothers were learning English at school," Grandma Beatrix said. "But Fatima and I wanted our own language, a code, so we created a third language."

"Yes," Fatima agreed with a nod. "But that's a story for another day . . . When we returned, the grasshoppers had been transformed into silver dollars. With one coin, the whole family could eat for more than a month. Eggs were a penny, bread three cents—a dollar meant a lot of food. We would've starved if we hadn't caught the insects our mother needed. Do you understand, little girl?"

Finishing my buñuelo, I nodded. I was grateful for not having to forage for food or touch winged critters. My grandparents and great-aunt were saints for not requiring much of me. I was expected to feed the house cats, water the lemon tree outside with the hose, and collect the mail, but that was it.

"And now we're old ladies," Grandma Beatrix bellowed. "We lived to tell the story of how we survived."

"What happened when your mother died?" I asked. "Who turned the grasshoppers into coins?"

Grandma Beatrix and Fatima met eyes. It seemed to me that their cheeks twitched with answers.

"The truth," Grandma Beatrix nodded solemnly as she continued in Spanish, "is that everyone is born knowing at least one spell. Some people know many—others even create new ones."

This was the first story and lesson they imparted to me, but over the course of our lives together, the stories multiplied until they were almost incalculable. The stories wallpapered my mind. Through them, I learned to shape myself. I dreamed and lived the stories without interruption. Alpha, omega, amen.

OF PESADILLAS, 1987

Sundays at mass, the same wanderer sat at the end of our pew. Unruly gray hair, striped linen shirt, black trousers, a hat on his lap. Without fail, he sought out my great-aunt Fatima's hand for the sign of the peace.

"Who is he?" I asked her one afternoon at home while we took turns filing each other's nails. It was clear he knew her from another vector or realm.

"Don't talk about him," she hushed, clicking her tongue.

Already, Fatima had observed me turning off radios with my mind, overhead lights. Occurrences I had not exerted energy to hide.

Nights later, I intercepted Fatima in her dreams. We lingered in front of my grandparents' house, the sky musky with secrets. A business envelope rested securely in her hands. My adolescent naivety failed to recognize the ritual of initiation.

She warned me, before turning away, "He's coming to meet me. It's best you leave."

The back of her head, a maze of black zigzags, pointed to future generations.

FATIMA, MIDSTRIDE, CIRCA 1988

Maybe I was ten when I snapped the unfocused photograph. The rectangular image bears no date, only the word Kodak slanted across the back. The subject is my great-aunt Fatima midstride on the sidewalk in front of my grandparents' house. Her facial expression is neutral, and a plastic bag hangs from her wrist.

After years of living with my grandparents, Fatima moved into a subsidized apartment down the block. Every morning, she arrived as the newspaper was being tossed onto the lawn and returned home after Dan Rather gave the evening news.

Summer mornings, she and I crocheted potholders while watching *The Price is Right*. We folded laundry, fed my grandmother's cats, and read paperbacks purchased at rummage sales.

Midway through July, Fatima suffered a heart attack in the living room while writing a letter to the mayor. She was distressed over the rising price of bus fare.

FATIMA, MIDSTRIDE, CIRCA 1988

After paramedics revived her on our rug, she propped herself up against the couch and chided the cats circled around, asking which of them wanted spankings.

The photograph is a grainy side profile of her on the sidewalk en route back to her apartment. I was frantic when I rushed outside with my slim 110 camera. I collected every detail about Fatima because her heart couldn't be trusted beneath her crocheted blankets at night.

Intuition told me I would outlive everyone—Fatima, my grandparents, Dan Rather, the cats. I would be my own house.

ONE EARRING

When my parents' house was burglarized, the culprits broke our toilet seat and stole the streusel my mother had baked the evening before. Of course, they also overturned every piece of furniture in our two-story home and left with the wildest amalgamation of items. Our prehistoric TV was left behind, but our equally junky VHS player was snatched.

As my mother absorbed the torrential disarray around us, her shock transformed itself into a series of journalistic questions. "Why did this happen?" eventually switched into "Who would do this?" Even our whirling ceiling fan could not disperse my mother's sorrow.

From the kitchen, we called the police, then my father, who was obliviously hard at work in his office across the highway. Over the phone, my father's chain of cusses sounded like measured instructions he expected us to follow.

When the cops arrived, they searched our house for clues. Our windows were dusted for fingerprints, though our busted back door was irrefutable proof of forced entry. One policeman stayed with us as we sifted through the rooms, while the other drove off in his shiny cruiser.

Upstairs, my room was the only one not bulldozed. Although my pillows were stripped bare, my stuffed animals had been rearranged with careful hands. The plush creatures faced forward, mute witnesses faintly smelling of strangers. Under a stack of my ugliest t-shirts, my heart-shaped diary remained locked and untouched.

In my parents' bedroom, I puzzled over the fact that the burglar had stolen a single earring from each pair in my mother's jewelry box. All these jewels were gifts my grandparents had given her before I existed. Heirlooms cruelly split in half. On the floor, I kneeled, foolishly searching for the other gold sand dollar, feeling for the missing Tahitian pearl.

When my father eventually arrived, I sprinted outside to greet him and unexpectedly exploded into tears. The policeman followed close behind me.

"Good evening," the officer said to my father. "How're you doing today?"

My father's face scrunched up with frustration as he spit out his reply.

"Great—until I learned my family had been burglarized. Now my daughter's hysterical. Pretend you're here to help, would you?"

Only as my father guided me through the plundered labyrinth of our house did I start to grasp the gravity of the attack: our home, possibly our family, had been targeted. The neighbors claimed to have seen nothing, yet they were not the least bit rattled by the prospect that they could be next. They were, in fact, never next.

That night, my father slept in front of our busted door with a wooden baseball bat. He swore the thieves would return, but they never did.

The next day, my mother drove me to school in a sensitive silence. She had forgotten to apply lipstick or pack me a lunch, but I mentioned neither.

In homeroom, I contemplated telling my teacher about the burglary. Halfway to her desk, I turned back around. My hot cheeks meant I might sob soon. I knew the confession would not excuse me from P.E, so it would be for nothing; I would have to run laps all the same and exhaust myself with endless jumping jacks like everyone else.

During lunch, while my classmates ate, I gulped water from the drinking fountain in the library until my stomach sloshed like a full canteen. Alone on the playground, I slipped off one of my gold unicorn earrings, fingering its tiny, twisted horn.

It made sense to examine things while they were still intact.

BLOOD PAISLEYS, 1990

Do you remember when drive-by shootings were an epidemic in San Antonio? When in middle school, every morning you'd greet your gaggle of friends by saying, "You survived the bullets, you nasty gangbangers," and they replied with quips like, "Yeah, I'm thug like that," or "I was wearing my Crips colors, fool!"

Only you were all twelve-year-old private-school girls, scared by the local nightly news, sick by the body counts in the newspaper headlines. Some of you were Mexican-American; some of you were white. All of you were equally fascinated by your uncivilized city as you were by your newfound period blood. Whenever an errant blood paisley stained a skirt or gym shorts, the group issued a warning to the victim: "Vato, you been shot near the buttocks. Get help."

Gangs were the rage, initiations were never-ending, and you were held hostage in the prime of puberty. This was before you began describing hip-hop as iambic, before you seriously considered the idea of leaving San Antonio, years before you developed your insulated New England daydream. The prospect of staying in your bloody city, well, that was a chalk outline you could draw in your sleep.

SAD GIRL, 1992

The very first time your parents allow you to go out by yourself, two cholas almost kick your ass. You have agreed to meet a boy for a matinee. The two of you see *Chaplin* in black and white, share a tub of popcorn, and kiss in the dark. The boy's face is crusted with infected pimples, but you're willing to close your eyes because being independent for half a day is a victory.

After the film, you part ways with your date and exit the mall. Your parents instructed you to wait at the bus stop bench, so you sit, squinting under the sun when a fellow Chicana appears. Her hands are deep in the pockets of khakis she paired with a white polo and black Converse sneakers. She's wearing her school uniform, you figure, on a weekend. Her obvious red lipstick and bandana signal to you that, in fact, you're face to face with a chola. Her exhalations enter your lungs and you almost choke.

She side-eyes you before saying, "You see my friend over there?"

MATH FOR THE SELF-CRIPPLING

In a McDonald's parking lot a dozen feet away, a husky chola flicks two switchblades while glaring at you. Every cell in your body dilates.

"She thinks you were looking at her funny," the first chola says.

Your initial fear is your teeth, but they may jump you in unison to razorblade your face. Years ago, you naively assumed you'd escaped the barrio, but the barrio returned to find you. It's inconsequential that you now attend a private school on a merit scholarship.

"Nah," you insist. "I wasn't looking at nobody."

Your use of a double negative is a deliberate type of Hail Mary.

"You sure, sad girl?" the bully asks, tilting her head.

You nod. The cholas exchange a conspiratorial glance—a synchronicity you will remember forever. This gesture means you get to keep your original face, that your dentist will never be part of this equation. It will haunt you that you were chosen and spared at random.

When you finally escape into your New England college dream, you'll regard the memory of that afternoon like a fossil, examining its vertebrae under a microscope.

For your 20th birthday, you'll treat yourself to a 14-karat gold nameplate necklace, oversized gold bamboo hoops, and dragon blood lipstick. From the neck up, you'll pattern yourself after your tormentors, thrilled by your transformation and struck by how very long it's been since you were a sad girl.

THROUGH SOPHIA LOREN GLASSES

My mother and I were driving past an exclusive neighborhood called The Elms when I asked how I would know if I had slipped into insanity. Two months before, when I turned fourteen, my consciousness had expanded into a thousand-floor hotel. Inside every room, I encountered duplicates of myself, all devious masterminds.

"You're not crazy," she said, shaking her head. "I can tell."

The open windows of her tiny Toyota welcomed a hot breeze that ballooned her white blouse and made her tan arms resemble hot dogs.

"But is there a line?" I asked.

In my mind, I shuffled over a black and white checkered floor, a human chess piece in clunky black men's oxfords. I jerked myself over the board, puppeting myself from black square to black square.

"I can't say if it's a line, but I know you're overthinking things again, mija."

I imagined my mother massaging Grandma Beatrix's knuckles while explaining my whereabouts to her in Spanish: "She's locked up in an institution with others like her."

From behind her gigantic Sophia Loren glasses, my grandmother's eyes were certain to flutter with shock.

I jittered in my car seat. All my dreams lately spackled of black magic and upon waking I stayed convinced I was cloaked in curses. It was clear I had to glue myself together for others. I'd hunt for swaths of normalcy at my private school—graph new veins into my central nervous system—present myself without fracture or blemish.

"Do you have homework?" my mother asked. Her attempt at a distraction soured the air, so I didn't answer.

"Don't tell me you *really* think you're crazy," she said, turning for the first time to study my mood.

Her face echoed a soap opera. Her lipstick faded into last week. We had been driving in the same direction for entirely too long and our destination eluded me.

"Most crazy people don't even realize they're crazy—you know that, right?" my mother mumbled, holding a conversation with herself.

I imagined myself being escorted out of my high school in a straitjacket, a hundred peers witnessing my unraveling, all of them too stunned to snicker or attempt a joke.

My mother's eyes darted up toward the rearview mirror.

"I'm sometimes on a chessboard," I muttered, "and it doesn't look like I'm going to win."

We maintained a speed of 55 mph and drove for four more years without ever stopping.

RUBRIC FOR YOUR NEW ENGLAND COLLEGE EXPERIENCE, 1998

Your gay friend introduces you to Adam, a blonde German with a last name that sounds like a torture weapon. Together they convince you to joyride with them to the frozen lake a few miles from your college.

All three of you strip to your birthday suits and skate in sneakers on the dense ice of Lake Champlain. You have not shaved your legs or bothered with your bikini line in weeks. Still, you love nothing more than being nineteen and believing your life is a string of epiphanies.

On the ride back, you all drink from a three-liter bottle of Pepsi and play *Truth or Dare*. Your gay friend dares Adam to drive with his eyes closed for a full minute. When he accepts, you lie across the backseat and pretend to be nestled inside a metal cocoon.

In his dorm later that night, you and Adam strip again. You tell him too much about yourself and your family. It's been ages since you shared such intimate details with anyone except your gay friend.

MATH FOR THE SELF-CRIPPLING

Adam caresses your cheek and tells you about his ex named Story. You have no right to be jealous, but you flick his hand away and wish your name were equally as imaginative. After kissing you passionately for a quarter of an hour, Adam tells you his housekeeper and your family are from the same country. Although he says this factually like a phone number, you are deeply ashamed. You should have shaved off every whisper of hair.

Your clothes are flipped inside out, and the glow of the moon outlines them like scattered index cards. If you're taking notes, remember this mistake and never repeat it.

HUNGRY PARALLELOGRAM

It was the gentlest knock, but it roused me from my sleep. My father opened my bedroom door, inviting in a white parallelogram of light across the hardwood floor.

"The nursing home just called," he whispered.

A heavy frown bookended his jowls, and even with sleep veiling my face, I knew what this meant. The day before I had visited my great-aunt Fatima at the nursing home. We sat in the lobby discussing her plan to teach her roommate to read in English. Although she'd spent the majority of her life shampooing heads at a salon, Fatima had taught me to read as a child and was eager for a new student.

"Once she can read, we can share a newspaper subscription," Fatima explained, "instead of wasting our days on idiotic game shows. I've got too much left upstairs to be guessing car prices or how many A's are in *Raiders of the Lost Ark*." Next to me on a sofa, she bounced her index finger off her temple to indicate that more chapters lay ahead.

Numbness overtook my face. There were no days left for her to guess vowels, or read op-eds, or for me to obsess over boys instead of visiting her.

"Mija," my father murmured, lingering in the threshold. "She left in her sleep."

The parallelogram on the floor yellowed before engulfing my bed.

Lurching to my knees, I tried yanking my v-neck shirt off in rebellion but only trapped myself inside. Hands and arms held hostage by sturdy cotton, I rammed the nearest wall, attempting to black out. My father hugged my outline as I punched and cursed an invisible thief.

COASTAL CUNEIFORM

My therapist suggests sand therapy. It sounds Eastern, like bonsai art. I nod to indicate I am open for whatever.

"The goal," my therapist starts but halts. "I don't want to influence you, so I won't suggest goals. The idea," she corrects herself, "is that whatever is on your mind will come to the surface. You'll work through it in the landscape."

She uncovers an octagonal basin of blonde sand. The perimeter is painted turquoise to symbolize a pacific sky. Scattered on tables around the room are objects I can manipulate to create scenarios. My eyes scan the plastic people, miniature yet delicately balanced.

Among the rows of potential civilians are a bespectacled grandfather, a pig-tailed Asian girl, a pregnant redhead, and a Native American man in a wheelchair.

On the wall, a cabinet hangs open displaying extraneous figurines and baubles: gemstones, wooden ambulances, vintage marbles, tarnished coins, and rubbery bouquets. I stifle the urge to question how much of this crap came from

Happy Meals. Neither G.I. Joe nor perfumed ponies can heal me.

With a plastic comb, I methodically even the sand. My shoulders slacken. Like a tired giant, I exhale onto the shaven terrain. My breath imprints a half clover in the basin. This curled 3 is an error my therapist might mistake for a lead.

I review the surface like I'm studying a legal contract. There is nothing I want to add, not a superficial wave or an elderly Mexican-American woman in a nursing home waiting to see whether death or I will visit her first.

Regret is a cliff far from any office of help.

FUR OF MY INSECURITIES

It happened in a chocolatier in Barcelona called Xococ, or another word equally as distressing on the jaw. We were selecting caramel squares like they were prayers or baby names. Glossy chocolate candies stuffed in a satin-lined box.

My mind draws a blank on the next four or five minutes. I know we were approaching the register when our purchase was interrupted. You wandered off, in search of a bathroom or a bottle of water, or to stretch your legs—I can't recall which. It must have been for water. We never left each other's side during vacations, but I nodded okay.

Moments later, I found myself circling a plaza, killing time, stifling my panic. After eight empty minutes of skimming the crowd, my face started to tense, hot vulnerability pooling in my eyes. This was our last vacation, but it wasn't in the cards for you to leave me so unceremoniously in Spain. Three years together could not end with almost chocolates—promises abandoned in a jewelry box. The names of our unborn children rotted with sugar and carelessness.

We didn't carry phones abroad, nor had we created an emergency plan. I didn't have a room key on me, and my fragmented mind couldn't recall our hotel name or the direction back. If you returned, I vowed to ask for a key and never be this helpless again.

Four times I passed a bare flagpole, frowned at the green elephant graffiti marking a wall, and bargained with a fictitious deity. I was parched, too, yet I would never have wandered off, alone.

I had time to purchase postcards, but I feared you'd never find me if I ducked into a shop. Images of happiness could wait for another time. The bang of my loneliness echoed against the flagpole; my fraught face transposed itself onto the scribbled green elephant.

The dyslexic sign of the chocolatier intimidated me—a word my tongue and brain could not team up to pronounce. The shopkeeper, her hand resting on our selections, peered at me through the window as I lapped around the pavement. *We'll be right back*, I almost insisted to the wind. The word *we* mutating into warped jeers.

I scanned the sparse crowd for your flyaway black hair, that outward gait of yours, but everyone's legs excluded me, turned inward in their own monogamy. Finally, tired of pacing, I leaned against the flagpole. Cold metal greeted my spine.

FUR MY INSECURITIES

Teenagers in high-tops laughed at each other, jangling coins and belt chains. My breathing hopscotched with questions of how long I could stand still.

From behind a nun's habit, your carefree smile came into focus, your llama expression of ease. I told myself to stay quiet, not to call out to you in desperation, not to spill any tears. You approached me nonchalantly and asked me where to next. I tilted my chin toward you and suggested the Picasso Museum. Chilled from the pole, I'm sure you noticed the quiver in my answer. *Sure*, you said. But first you suggested I pose by the elephant graffiti. You were disturbingly new to me then, aiming our camera as I posed by the scrawled animal outline. My lipstick photographed as a ghostly berry ring and I raised two fingers into the peace sign.

Almost immediately we slipped back into our normal selves in Picasso's presence, discussing his pencil sketches and planning our evening meal: oysters with absinthe cocktails.

At nightfall we meandered back to our hotel, enjoying the air of an ancient city while ignoring the ominous echo of our boots on cobblestone. Each of our heels scribbled impossible kōans.

TABLOID TOTEMS

Your guilty pleasure for the past decade has been reading tabloids online. Splashed across your desktop screen are astronomically scaled photographs of popular and burnt-out celebrities. Since you can remember, a particular blonde male model has reminded you of your ex-boyfriend, also a model, but tall and Japanese. Except for their feathered eyebrows and similar clothing campaigns, the men are incongruent. Yet to you, they are as interchangeable as quickly scribbled fives and s's.

One November they appear in the same section of *The New York Times*. The blonde man models quixotic cologne; your ex poses pensively with platinum cufflinks. Flipping back and forth between the ads, you can't decide which man is yours. After a quiet hour of scrutiny, you ball up the paper and toss it into a public trash can.

Three blocks down Columbus Avenue, you buy a fresh copy of the newspaper you just discarded. A throbbing tightness spreads across the bridge of your nose as you realize you will never own them, only facsimiles of their silhouettes.

The reasons for your breakup with the model blur more with each season. You text your close friend and ask why you did it. It was years ago, and you doubt your motives and loathe your friends for not advising you to stick it out. Regret engulfs you like a heavy winter coat. *He was dragging you both down*, your friend replies. Another green bubble of text appears: *Don't forget the problems.* These oblique answers annoy you. You wonder if your ex misses you, if he saved the birthday cards you penned him, and if so, which ones.

In Paris, a deranged fan assaults the blonde model in front of a café. His bruised face, gigantic and unrecognizable, graces your desktop monitor. From work, you FaceTime your mother in hysterics.

"You won't believe what happened," you sob.

The model's face resembles a navy slab of meat, his eyelids swollen shut. The police arrived too late to save his magazine features. With hyphenated exhales you utter the blonde model's name over and over.

"You don't even know him," your mother fumes.

In your mind, you add the word *anymore* because for years you followed his photographs, and for quite some time you fell asleep next to, and dreamt of growing old with, someone like him.

HANDS ON METALLIC PONDS

Her religion is the power of suggestion. In the newspaper, she reads about the nanny who stabbed two children to death with a butcher knife before slitting her own throat. It happened on West 75th Street near Central Park, an area she knows rather well.

For weeks, she cannot stomach a knife without thinking of the stabbings. Wide blades glint like metallic ponds. Her kitchen fills with muted primal screams and virginal sunlight. It shudders with footsteps. She avoids the pull, orders take-out, and eats in a hallway armchair with clear plastic utensils.

As a troubled teen, when her parents reminded her of her dishwashing duties after dinner, she often envisioned whacking off one of her hands at the wrist with a meat cleaver. Retribution for forced labor. If she wielded it swiftly, she doubted she'd break the shock barrier. Five twitching fingers: a Halloween prop, or the salvage of her own digits?

HANDS ON METALLIC PONDS

In adulthood, knives continue to haunt her. She considers therapy to tame these disturbing impulses, but she's careful not to taint others with knife romance.

In metallic ponds, minnows convulse like nervous blood cells. Beneath the surface, a Loch Ness lurks in search of believers.

SHORT ANSWERS

The therapist asks about my first memory of despair. This is too easy: a multiple-choice question with the correct answers listed as a), b), c), and d). I reply with a wince— Sunday afternoons of my youth spent in my parents' living room, dust atoms arrested in sunlight, newspaper strewn about, and the judgmental remnants of Sunday mass percolating within me. This was my primer, my first lesson in vanishing hope.

What about your current state of despair, the therapist asks. It's true these emotions have matured from zygotes into adults. They've lost teeth, outgrown their braids and mohawks, sat for yearbook pictures, worked crap jobs, fought with lovers, and concocted plans to end the flipbook of my life. Yet even when prompted, I am reluctant to measure the depth of their reservoir, to acknowledge the sedimentary layers of their helplessness.

The therapist invites me to imagine my life without this oppressive burden. She is testing my loyalty, determining whether I possess the fortitude to bury my own. Yet it will never be a simple matter of tossing fresh bouquets on graves and letting go. Instead, it would require a massive undertaking, encyclopedias full of birth and death certificates, three shifts of gravediggers, and endless sweat and surrender.

Within a month, I'll forget the therapist's name, the waiting room couches, the wall art hinting at new beginnings.

LAST CHAPTER ON HOTEL STATIONERY

It's 4 a.m. in Zagreb, Croatia, and you're wide-awake. You and your husband are on your honeymoon. While he sleeps, you admire his black curly hair and thin nose, envious of his ability to rest. As he rotates to his side, you wonder what images are crossing his unconscious mind and whether he's ferried a phantom of you into his dreams.

Jet lag has left your body disoriented, so you mime resting poses. You've read more than once that lost sleep can never be recaptured. This fact concerns you, and you're almost compelled to wake Marcelo to even the tally. You're in this together now, and some part of you hopes you die together for the sake of simplicity.

By 5 a.m., you can't take it anymore. You get up from bed and drink the bottled water you purchased at Charles de Gaulle airport during your transfer. The minibar tempts you, but you're already dehydrated, and Jack Daniels will only worsen your case. You pop a few aspirin, pretending they're sedatives, but you and sleep continue to skirt each other like foes.

From the floor-to-ceiling windows in your hotel room, periwinkle light begins to seep in. You hear garbage trucks roam and stop on the street below. You welcome the symphony of labor but know the noise will only prolong your descent into dreams.

Across from your hotel stands an imposing building called Institut Français de Zagreb. Next to it is an Adidas boutique, and adjacent is what you presume to be an eyewear shop. The window displays an overexposed photo of an androgynous face sporting hot pink Ray-Bans. The face in the window reminds you of your model ex-boyfriend Hiroshi.

While vacationing with Hiroshi once in Barcelona, you recognized his profile on a United Colors of Benetton ad at a train stop. At home in Manhattan, you routinely saw his face—ravine-sharp cheekbones and punk rocker hair—sail by on crosstown buses. At first it was disarming for you to encounter jumbo-sized images of your lover traversing the city, but soon every replica reinforced the magnitude of your connection to him. You'd chosen well and the evidence was pixelated for the public.

That was years ago. Your life now feels less exciting. Although there were plenty of bad times, you pine for billboard illusions over this tethered tiredness.

You wonder if marriage is the last chapter. You're glad Marcelo's eyes are shut because you already doubt your union with him. Bringing your left hand to your face, you rub your wedding band and engagement ring over your lips in a rough, unreciprocated kiss.

You squint out the window and hate Croatia. Later in the day, you'll feel exhausted by the time change, by the rude, old Croats who'll discriminate against you and your husband because of your dark complexions. You'll wish you had honeymooned in Bali, or New Zealand, or someplace farther that you couldn't afford.

By 6 a.m., you feel like a mollusk confined inside an unforgiving shell. You're convinced this predicament is to blame for your short stature and mental straitjacket. For the second time, you consider the private fiesta of the minibar but quickly dismiss the impulse.

In the bathroom, you brush your teeth again in the dark. As you exit, you clumsily bang your leg against the metal trashcan under the sink. You're sure you'll wake Marcelo when you scream shit in Spanish, but you don't. He continues to sleep like he's been drugged for surgery.

Before you married him, you told Marcelo you'd never wanted kids. You were dead serious, and you will be until you're just dead. He said he was fine with that. As you cross the carpet from the bathroom back to the bed, you

LAST CHAPTER ON HOTEL STATIONERY

wish you'd requested a polygraph to confirm his answer and everything else the two of you exchanged with such certainty.

You study the face in the Ray-Ban ad then lie down next to your husband. Faces, you've heard, morph. In years to come, people at parties will comment that you and Marcelo look alike, that you resemble two Siamese cats, and a slew of other drunken inanities, none of which are true. On this bed tonight you're reduced to a bruise of solitude.

You blink sharply at the outline of your suitcases, the desk replete with hotel stationery. Despite the fact that you've never drawn with any level of accuracy, you're compelled to diagram the abrupt shift your life took yesterday—from carefree cartoon to this crushing checkmate.

THE EQUIVALENT OF _____

On the last full day of our honeymoon, Marcelo and I boarded a public bus to a casino located inside a mall. We'd been fighting, so it hadn't occurred to us how vacant a casino would be at three in the afternoon. The sight of only a few truant teenagers loitering in front of the complex sobered us and confirmed our knack for bad decisions.

We had never been to Vegas, yet it was obvious this was a poor excuse for a casino. Aside from aisles of shiny red and gold slot machines, the interior was reminiscent of a pizza parlor arcade. Under a canopy of blinking lights, waxen-looking staff stood dressed in pressed, white-collared shirts and black slacks. Marcelo and I avoided each other's eyes while feeding the noisy machines. The number of awful or disappointing experiences we'd encountered on our honeymoon was approaching a fucking hundred.

After losing the equivalent of fifteen American dollars straightaway, we decided to comb the rest of the mall for cultural oddities. Since learning the modern-day tie originated in Croatia, we'd half-heartedly decided to find two or three stylish ones for Marcelo. The only thing was Marcelo was indifferent to ties, so we idled about hoping to stumble upon specialty candies or newfangled household gadgets.

After strolling past a budget beauty shop and an artificial flower boutique, we entered a battery repair shop with two display cases of silver jewelry. Marcelo and I both knew this mall, bleak and ill-conceived, was a living portrait of us.

With a spark of optimism, he said, "I'll buy you anything you want here."

My watch still ticked, but I sensed he was trying, so I stifled a snort. This was possibly the first time either one of us had attempted tenderness in five days.

Standing in front of a revolving stand, I inspected heart-shaped sterling silver charms and zigzag pins that had been popular in the United States circa 1987. Bad jewelry, I realized, is universal. Nothing remotely appealed to me.

The shop owner detected my apathy. He curled his finger for me to approach then retrieved a velvet-lined tray from under the register.

Rows of crude and chintzy earrings lined the tray like elongated fish. In the center rested the most promising pair: silver coins roped onto silver hooks. Kenzo, a brand I only recognized as a perfume manufacturer, was stamped on the back of each silver disc.

"Do you want them?" Marcelo asked. "Can she try them on?" he asked the owner.

The elderly man nodded with closed eyelids as if to indicate this was all scripted.

I tucked my hair behind my earlobes and slid the earrings in. The roped coins grazed my jawline and refracted in the mirror.

Marcelo appeared over my shoulder, the curve of his smile nearly lost in his overgrown beard. The thought *I hope we never divorce* formed like a fence in my mind, and although everything about the mall, Croatia, and us felt doomed, I truthfully confessed, "I love them."

Under ordinary circumstances this might have marked a peace. But the next day, we squabbled on the flight out of Zagreb and barked sarcasms at each other while racing to catch our connection in Dublin. We left barbs and blame in every country, on half-eaten meals, balled up inside receipts, our graffiti on everything.

MACROSCOPIC SACRED PUZZLES

The day my husband starts wearing glasses, he begins a comprehensive investigation of all things optic. At 28, his corneas are seared by the miniature image of a juicy hamburger on a coupon. With gusto, he admires the pyramidal composition of his screensaver—two monkeys aloft a tree limb—noting, for the first time, that the Dijon-hued monkey is an infant.

My husband's reverence for every organism and manmade structure is touching yet tiring. On a long drive, he rhapsodizes about the commanding font of highway signs. Later, he is rendered speechless by the lush spectral streak of sports cars torpedoing past us.

Back home, he squints from behind his frames, scrutinizing our wall décor. One surrealistic black and white poster is a lonely tourist from my adolescence. He studies this relic of my lost faith: a gothic cathedral with city traffic filing down the pews.

Between his eyelashes, no puzzle piece is trivial. Every atom equals a garden.

THE POSTURE OF A GENTLEMAN

She hates it. Her stuffed animal is aging. The day she and her husband bought him near Trevi Fountain in Rome, the monkey's russet fabric was taut. Its alert features exemplified the mark of craftsmanship. It never crossed her mind that the monkey would age and wrinkle, or that the cotton stuffing would shift and disintegrate.

When she leaves her apartment, she props him up with pillows and crosses his legs, mimicking the posture of a gentleman. She's painstaking about keeping him out of the sun, away from cigarette smoke, off the floor, and free of lint.

As a child she regularly visited garage sales with her great-aunt Fatima and Grandma Beatrix. On strangers' lawns, she would gaze upon mountains of spoiled and forsaken stuffed animals, each matted with toddler drool or disfigured by partially melted Jolly Ranchers. The mounds of toys reeked of fevers, sad houses, and junk food. By age six, she had trained herself to avert her eyes from the piles, praying she wouldn't gag in public.

THE POSTURE OF A GENTLEMAN

Her husband teases her now, says she'll have a nervous breakdown if anything were to happen to the monkey. Something is happening to the monkey, imperceptibly, day by day. His football-shaped head has begun to tilt southward; his parallel legs are hollowing out. Her devotion is consuming him one thread at a time.

EFFIGIES OF OURSELVES

I say, "Let's do it."

You say you have to smoke first. You go outside with your pack of cigarettes and lighter.

I get comfortable on the couch and begin reading a short story.

You come back inside and say you're ready.

I hold up a hand and say, "Five more minutes."

You say you'll shower in the meantime. Down the hallway you sulk. The water jerks on, and I finish the story with time to kill.

I wash a few plates sitting in the sink, a fork and a knife.

You walk into the kitchen with wet hair, faded boxers, bare feet, and that orphan frown. "Okay," I say, "I'll be right there."

When I meet you in the bedroom, you're watching stand-up comedy on TV.

"Now?" I ask.

"Three minutes, just three minutes," you cackle with cruel laughter.

This is how we build resentments. This is why I don't even want to touch you. When you're finally ready, I'm so fed up with the wait, your sulking, our excuses; I'm ready to build a bonfire of your cigarettes.

MUIR BEACH

We wake at an ungodly hour to meditate with the monks in the mountains. We prepare for uninterrupted silence by feasting on piercing piano sonatas and inwardly laughing at the joke that most lapsed Catholics are open to Buddhism.

San Quentin Prison gleams to our left as we near our destination, and the San Francisco Bay quivers platinum around us. The drive up the mountain is precarious, so we yield for bicyclists. We are considerate of skulls coated in helmets, bare legs, human muscle versus automotive machinery.

In the Zen Center, we bow to each other, sit, and concentrate on our breathing. Our chests expand to envelop everyone in the room. Our chests contract to self-forgive. After the gong is struck, we file out to sip tea, change shoes, and begin the trek to Muir Beach.

Poison ivy and daunting inclines greet us at the start of the trail. The hike is Herculean and tests us for hours. We murmur complaints, but the vistas romance our retinas.

Miles later the mountain begins to slope downward. The

rocks beneath us are loose, a foundation unraveling unto itself. We angle ourselves sideways to descend smoothly and are thrust into a frigid curtain of wind.

On level terrain, we bundle ourselves in pashminas before unlacing our sneakers. We trudge barefoot over the black speckled sand and weave our way through paddle ball games. Children prance around us half naked in pastel bikinis and trunks, immune to the cold.

Along the coast, we negotiate our bodies like meter markers. We momentarily forget that one of us is ill, that this entire day was prescribed as medicine.

Glass waves lap over our bare feet, an icy rush of grainy sediment. We lock eyes like we did at the beginning, before our words tangled and thorned us.

One spell is complete.

MATH FOR THE SELF-CRIPPLING

When my day is irrevocably ruined, I drive by my childhood house. Painted evergreen and cream, the exterior has shifted faces like waves have rearranged coastal sands.

To maim myself, I pretend this address is still mine. This is the plot of land where I learned to read, where we were burglarized, where my parents and I sang happy birthday three times a year, where my mother tripped down a dozen stairs, where I alchemized our lives into poetry, and where my father cursed our debt. I hold on like a Doberman to a museum of us.

The tunnel of my teens could not fathom strangers gathered around our fireplace or children scowling into our bathroom mirrors. An anonymous family mimes their life through open curtains.

Projections of the unfamiliar return me to the driver's seat.

This house never taught me how to let go. My parents and

MATH FOR THE SELF-CRIPPLING

I are still singing, reading, screaming, writing, falling. We have not yet unhung the photos from the walls or ripped the sheets off the beds. I am still hunched over the dinner table, fretting over math.

HUSBAND IN TRANSLATION

He returns every evening at 6 p.m. and asks if I've found a job yet. I have a part-time job, but it isn't enough. My husband expects me to work in a respectable office and wear high heels every day. He has a fantasy of meeting at a pub for happy hour, both of us exhausted and full of work drama. Our twin martinis escape valves, long-stemmed sour tonics.

The climate in the apartment escalates until I dread 6 p.m., the question, my shrug that betrays indifference.

"I applied to two more jobs today," I sometimes volunteer.

"When you're looking for a job, applying *becomes* your job. Why are you not treating it like a job?"

"Well," I explain, "because I work part-time and often marinate chicken when I get home, so we can eat dinner together."

After a string of identical weeks, my dreams become strange theater soliloquies. On stage, I reflect and rage, a blinding spotlight tracking my every step.

HUSBAND IN TRANSLATION

Our bills bulk into bullies, so I continue to apply for more office jobs. Positions to answer phones, update databases, interact with professors, delegates, or philanthropists. I write impeccable cover letters, brimming with enthusiasm, yet no one calls. Occasionally I receive emails informing me that [*company name*] is no longer pursing my candidacy. Such notices elate and panic me. This means the road ahead is endless: more applications, cover letters, hours robbed from my day.

Throughout my life, I've had many full-time jobs, though never in an office. My best position was as a museum curator in Buenos Aires. As the only fully bilingual employee, I was often intercepted and asked to translate.

Q: "How do you say tacones?"

A: "High heels."

Q: "How do you say un marido fastidioso?"

A: "Annoying husband."

Q: "How do you say déjame en paz?"

A: "Get off my back."

MASTERPIECES

I buy myself a new pillow every time I get a raise. It is a bijou luxury. My employer is a whirling institution that swallows my hours. Each week is a blur of wooden doors I enter and exit, and electronic correspondences I type at top speed. My supervisors stress over departmental budgets, and my colleagues commiserate about meetings from hell. *In the grand scheme of life,* I am tempted to shout, *a job is a footnote. It is a means, not a Michelangelo.*

My evenings are a hush. Dinners of meat and vegetables, and an atlas spread across the table. I have visited seventeen countries. My eyes have beheld the Iguazu Falls, the Coliseum, the Taj Mahal, Mycenaean pottery, and animals of every persuasion. On my couch, I sip white tea from a demitasse cup and plot my next jaunt.

Like clockwork, fatigue guides me to bed. I earn the pillows. It is emancipating to test them at the store. To place my head against a TRY ME sample. It is a limbo between freedom and coffin.

ABACUS OF SELF-IMPROVEMENT

Quit telling your coworkers that you dreamt them last night. You've been entering dreams since you were nine. Occasionally, you suspect osmosis, that you are fluidly entering each other's membranes to transmit office rumors, nefarious budget secrets, details about whose retirement is growing stout like a hog. You used to eat pennies per month until the dreams wised you up. You now devour Thousand Layer Cake and avenge until your eyes part in the morning.

Listen: You must quit announcing the dreams, quit referencing them like canonical literature. Keep your blue tongue hidden and all your meditations, too. Privacy is a figment of Eden—a utopia erased.

From church pews through marriage and in quiet offices, they pursue you like leopards with their breath. Deliver no envelopes. Trust no man.

ACKNOWLEDGEMENTS

Several writers provided valuable feedback that helped improve this book. Among the most vital are Eleanor Henderson and Pablo Piñero Stillmann. Over the years, many friends sustained me with their unwavering support and often asked how the writing was going. Some writers prefer not to be asked about their progress, but I found it heartening to be so encouraged. For that reason, I give thanks to the following people: Miriam Elman, Mohit Praful Mehta, Evan Mallon, Melissa Kozak, T Kira Madden, Hannah Beresford, Brian Morton, Steve Edwards, Robert James Russell, Pam Kingsbury, Rubén Degollado, Roma Kaul, Melissa R. Sipin, Jennifer Schooley, Sebastian Páramo, Nicholas Duron, Justine Champine, Lilly Gonzalez, Noah Bloem, Suleman Hussain, Jose Diaz, Sara Ronis, Kaustubh Thakur, Rheaclare Fraser-Spears, Keith Spears, Marques Brooks, Barry Duncan, Zack Bond, Chris Garcia, and Virginia Laque.

Thank you to the editors who originally gave these pieces the right home, and in some cases a second life, including

Megan Giddings, Scott Garson, Elle Nash, Matt Sailor, Leesa Cross-Smith, Matthew Salesses, Bükem Reitmayer, Aaron Burch, and Roxane Gay.

Huge thanks for Gold Line Press for publishing this magical project of mine. I'm indebted to Zinzi Clemmons for selecting this manuscript as the fiction winner. It's been a pleasure working with the Gold Line staff, particularly Krishna Narayanamurti and Sam Cohen. Sandra Rosales, you gave me my absolute dream cover—thank you!

Thanks to Mrs. Suzanne Elizondo of Keystone School for telling me I was a writer when I was barely eleven or twelve. I believed her, and good things followed.

My heart is full of gratitude to Manuel and Sylvia Villarreal for always encouraging me to write and create all the enchanting things born of my imagination. Endless thanks to Fernando Moura for carving a life with me that allows me to write and obsess and rewrite and perfect my stories and books.

Earlier versions of many pieces first appeared in literary journals: Origin, 1983 in *Paper Darts*; Envelope First, 1953 and Of Pesadillas, 1987 as Rosicrucian Triptych in *CutBank*; Fatima, midstride, circa 1988 in *Jelly Bucket*; One Earring in *Corium*; Blood Paisleys, 1990 and Tabloid Totems in *The Emerson Review*; Blood Paisleys, 1990 reprinted in *TAYO*; Tabloid Totems reprinted in *Columbia Journal*; Sad Girl, 1992 and Through Sophia Loren Glasses in *Wigleaf*; Rubric for Your New England College Experience, 1998 in *NANO Fiction* and reprinted in *TAYO*; Fur of My Insecurities in *Lunch Ticket*; Hands on Metallic Ponds in *Black Heart Magazine*; Short Answers and Effigies of Ourselves in *DOGZPLOT*; Last Chapter on Hotel Stationery in *The Toast*; The Equivalent of _____ in *WhiskeyPaper* and reprinted in *Forward: 21st Century Flash Fiction*; Macroscopic Sacred Puzzles in *The Doctor T.J. Eckleburg Review*; The Posture of a Gentleman in *Atticus Review*; Muir Beach in *Folio*; Math for the Self-Crippling in *Literary Orphans*; Husband in Translation in *Cosmonauts Avenue*; Masterpieces in The Normal School; Abacus of Self-Improvement in *Hobart*.

Ursula Villarreal-Moura was born and raised in San Antonio, Texas. Her stories, essays, interviews, and reviews have appeared in various publications including *Tin House*, *Catapult*, *Prairie Schooner*, *Story*, *Midnight Breakfast*, *Gulf Coast*, and *Bennington Review*. Her writing has been nominated for *Best of the Net*, the Pushcart Prize, *Best Small Fictions*, and one of her stories was listed as distinguished in *Best American Short Stories* 2015.